THE ARABIAN NIGHTS
CHILDREN'S COLLECTION

Dados Internacionais de Catalogação na Publicação (CIP) de acordo com ISBD

J76a   Jones, Kellie
        Ali Baba and the forty thieves / adaptado por Kellie Jones. – Jandira : W. Books, 2025.
        112 p. ; 12,8cm x 19,8cm. – (The Arabian nights)

        ISBN: 978-65-5294-176-3

        1. Literatura infantojuvenil. 2. Contos. 3. Contos de Fadas. 4. Literatura Infantil.
        5. Clássicos. 6. Mágica. 7. Histórias. I. Título. II. Série.

2025-601   CDD 028.5
                                                            CDU 82-93

Elaborado por Vagner Rodolfo da Silva - CRB-8/9410
Índice para catálogo sistemático:
1. Literatura infantojuvenil 028.5
2. Literatura infantojuvenil 82-93

The Arabian Nights 10 Book Collection
Text © Sweet Cherry Publishing Limited, 2023
Inside illustrations © Sweet Cherry Publishing Limited, 2023
Cover illustrations © Sweet Cherry Publishing Limited, 2023

Text based on translations of the original folk tale,
adapted by Kellie Jones
Illustrations by Sarah Grace

© 2025 edition:
Ciranda Cultural Editora e Distribuidora Ltda.

1st edition in 2025
www.cirandacultural.com.br
No part of this publication may be reproduced, stored in a retrieval
system, or transmitted in any form or by any means, electronic,
mechanical, photocopying, recording, or otherwise, without written
permission of the publisher.
This book is a work of fiction. Names, characters, places, and incidents
are either the product of the author's imagination or are used fictitiously,
and any resemblance to actual persons, living or dead, business
establishments, events, or locales is entirely coincidental.

Ali Baba
and the
Forty Thieves

W. Books

Long ago, in the ancient lands of Arabia, there lived a brave woman called Scheherazade. When the country's sultan went mad, Scheherazade used her cleverness and creativity to save many lives – including her own. She did this over a thousand and one nights, by telling the sultan stories of adventure, danger and enchantment.

This is just one of them …

Ali Baba
A poor woodcutter

Cassim
Ali Baba's richer brother

Esme
Ali Baba's wife

Soraya
Cassim's wife

Morgiana
A clever servant

The Leader of the Forty Thieves
A dangerous man

Adeem & Yusef
Thieves in disguise

Baba Mustapha
An old cobbler

Salil
Ali Baba's son

Chapter 1

In a dusty town in Syria, between desert and forest, there lived two brothers. One brother was called Cassim and the other was called Ali Baba.

When their father died, the brothers divided what little he had owned between them and were equals. But soon after Cassim married a very rich woman and became a wealthy merchant. Meanwhile Ali Baba married a woman as poor as himself and lived by cutting wood.

One day, Ali Baba was working in the forest and had cut enough wood to load his three donkeys with. He had no cart so he was preparing to walk them into town to sell it when he saw a great cloud of dust in the distance that was growing closer and closer. He watched until he realised that the dust was caused by many men on horseback riding towards him.

Fearing that the men might attack

merchant
Someone who buys and sells goods.

him, Ali Baba hid his donkeys behind a huge, craggy rock. Then he hid himself up in a tall, thick tree. From its branches, he watched their arrival. He counted forty men in total, all carrying weapons and riding horses with bulging saddlebags. The bags were so heavy that the men struggled to lift them. As they did, a few gold coins fell to the ground.

They must be robbers, thought Ali Baba. *But what are they doing here?*

As he watched, a large, bearded man who appeared to be the leader walked up to the rock and said: 'Open sesame!' To Ali Baba's astonishment, a door immediately opened in the rock. Through it the leader entered, followed by his thirty-nine men and their saddlebags. The door closed behind them.

The robbers stayed for some time inside the rock, during which Ali Baba remained in the tree. At last all forty men came out again. Only now their saddlebags were empty.

'Shut sesame!' said the leader. The door shut.

Ali Baba watched as the men mounted their horses and rode away, kicking up as much dust as they arrived with. Then he climbed out of the tree.

Ali Baba walked up to the rock, which looked so smooth and solid that he almost thought he had imagined the door. He could see no trace of it.

'Open … sesame?' he said.

The door instantly appeared.

Inside the rock, Ali Baba expected to find a dark, dank cave, so he was surprised by the well-lit, spacious chamber that greeted him. Sunlight poured in through an opening in the

ceiling, too high up to be seen from
the ground outside. It shone down
on all sorts of treasures, from
bales of silk, glittering brocade
and the finest woven carpets piled
atop one another, to gold and

silver coins in great heaps and overflowing bags.

Boldly, Ali Baba collected as much gold as his three donkeys could carry. Afterwards he laid chopped wood over the bags to hide them. When he was done, he said, 'Shut sesame!' and led the animals home. There he emptied the bags of gold before his wife, Esme. The heaps dazzled her eyes and all she wanted to know was where he had found such riches.

'We must keep this treasure a secret,' she said, after he had told

brocade
A fabric with a raised, woven pattern.

her. 'The thieves might try to take it back otherwise.'

'I will dig a hole and bury it. There is no time to be lost.'

'First let me count it.'

'That will take too long!'

'Then let me fetch your brother's scales to weigh it.'

So Ali Baba started digging and Esme went to Cassim's house. Cassim's wife, Soraya, answered.

'What could you possibly have to weigh?' Soraya asked when she had heard Esme's request.

'Oh, um, just some rice,' Esme replied vaguely.

Soraya narrowed
her eyes suspiciously.
For years now she
had enjoyed being
richer than her
sister-in-law. She
never missed a
chance to say how much better her
husband was than his brother. It
was on the tip of her tongue now
to say: 'Ali Baba can barely afford
enough rice to feed you! Why
would you need to weigh it?'

But she went to fetch the
scales as asked. Before handing
them over, however, she secretly

smeared soft candle wax at the bottom of the weighing plate. *That way,* she thought, *whatever they weigh will stick to the plate, and I will know what it* really *was.*

'There you go,' she said when she was done. 'Bring them back as soon as you are finished with them.'

Back at home, of course, it was not rice that Esme weighed but gold. Measure upon measure of gold. When she was done, she helped Ali Baba to bury it all. Afterwards she returned the scales to Soraya. She was so tired from all the digging that she failed to notice a single gold coin stuck to the wax. Soraya, of course, *did* notice.

'Cassim, look at this,' she said, showing the coin to her husband who was in his counting house.

'Where did you get that?'

'It seems your brother and his wife have more gold than they can count. They have to weigh it!' Just the idea made her jealous. 'How can a woodcutter have more gold than a merchant? Especially a merchant who is married to *me*!

Where is all our money?'

'It is right here!' Cassim said, waving a hand at the neatly stacked coins before him. He had been in the middle of counting when Soraya appeared.

'Exactly!' she sneered. 'A child could count this much. Ali Baba must be far richer than you.'

A better brother would have been pleased to learn that Ali Baba's fortunes had changed. But Cassim was as mean as his wife, and soon he was just as jealous as her too. He could not sleep at all that night and went to Ali Baba's house before sunrise.

Ali Baba had hardly seen his brother since he married Soraya and became rich. He was surprised to see him now.

'Ali Baba,' Cassim greeted him, 'I am surprised at you. You pretend to be poor and yet you have gold to weigh. My wife found this at the bottom of the scales you borrowed yesterday. Why did Esme lie and say you were weighing rice?'

'I am sure Esme did not mean to lie, brother. She probably did not know what else to say. I found this gold only yesterday, you see, and we do not want it to be discovered.'

'Discovered by whom?' Cassim demanded. 'Where did you find it?'

So Ali Baba told his brother all about the thieves and the rock and the secret passphrase.

'And you say there is more treasure still left in the cave?' Cassim asked. 'You did not take it all?'

'I did not need to! Three donkeys-worth is plenty.'

'Not as much as *six* donkey's worth. What did you say the passphrase was? Open chickpea?'

'Open *sesame*,' Ali Baba corrected him. 'But be careful, brother, the more treasure you take, the more likely the thieves will notice it missing.'

Cassim was already walking away from his brother's simple hut, towards his own grand house. 'You just want it for yourself!' he shouted back over his shoulder.

Early the next morning, Cassim was ready to set out for the forest when Soraya stopped him.

'Why do you have six donkeys?' she asked.

'Because my brother only had three.'

'Are you only twice the man Ali Baba is? I say you are *three times* the man! Take *nine* donkeys!'

So Cassim set off with nine donkeys, each carrying great chests that he intended to fill with treasure. He followed the road that Ali Baba had told him about, and it was not long before he reached the huge, craggy rock.

'It looks completely solid,' Cassim said to himself. 'No sign of a door at all! Ali Baba better not have lied to me …' He cleared his throat. Feeling silly, he said: 'Open sesame?'

Immediately a door appeared and opened wide. As Cassim entered the cave, the door closed behind him. Once again, there was plenty of light to see the treasures inside, but Cassim wasted no time enjoying the sight of them. He quickly laid as many bags of riches as he could carry at the invisible door of the cave. Then he said, 'Open chickpea.'

Nothing happened.

'Open barley!'

No door appeared.

Cassim's thoughts were now so full of money that he had

forgotten the passphrase.

'Open corn! Open wheat! Open rice! OPEN!'

But only the words "open sesame" would work. Without them, Cassim was trapped.

Chapter 2

Angrily, Cassim threw down the money and jewels he was still holding. He punched a rolled carpet. He kicked a mound of diamond jewellery. He slipped and fell on a broken string of pearls. Then Cassim lay on his back and stared up at the hole in the top of the cave, through which sunlight spilled.

… *Maybe I can climb out*, he thought.

But when Cassim tried to scale the cave walls, he found himself falling flat on his back again. And again. And again. Until one fall seemed to shake the whole cave.

As Cassim sat up painfully, the loose pearls on the ground trembled and rolled. Piles of gold coins shifted and spilled. Then he heard horse hooves – dozens of them.

Forty of them.

From a distance, the thieves had seen Cassim's donkeys tied up outside their cave. Now they galloped at full speed towards it.

Desperately, Cassim tried again to open the door. 'Open buckwheat! Open maize! Open flax!'

By the time the thieves arrived, Cassim could not think of any more grains.

Outside the cave, nine thieves checked the nine donkeys.

'The chests are empty.'

Thirty thieves checked the area.

'There is no one out here.'

And the leader eyed the rock.

'Open sesame!'

The moment the door opened, Cassim charged at the thieves. 'AAAAAARGH!' he yelled, hoping to startle the thieves and escape. Instead, he ran straight onto their swords and was cut to pieces.

The leader stared at the dead body, annoyed. 'You idiots! Now we cannot ask him how he knew about this place or how to get in!'

'Or if he was alone,' another thief added.

The leader shoved him into the cave. 'So go see if anything is missing!'

'Several bags of gold are gone,' he was told after some counting.

'Either this was not the first time he has stolen from us, or he has an accomplice,' the leader

accomplice
A person who helps someone do something even though they know it is a crime.

decided. 'Leave his body here as a warning just in case.'

So the thieves left Cassim's body where it had fallen, closed the cave and rode away.

At home his wife Soraya waited in vain for him to return. When evening came but he did not, she was so worried that she went to Ali Baba.

'Cassim still has not returned from the forest,' she said, pacing back and forth across her brother-in-law's tiny home. 'Something must have happened to him.'

'Or he waited for darkness to hide

the treasure he brings back with him,' Ali Baba reassured her. 'I am sure he is on his way home now.'

This made sense to Soraya. Cassim would want to keep the treasure a secret, after all, and the quieter, nighttime streets would be better for that.

But when Soraya returned home, hours continued to pass without any sign of her husband. Slowly her fear grew greater than her greed. By midnight she thoroughly regretted learning about the treasure and sending Cassim after it. By morning she was back at Ali Baba's house.

'Go and look for him!' she demanded. 'Bring him home!'

'I will go,' he promised, 'but please do not worry about Cassim. I am sure he is fine.'

'I am not worried about Cassim! I am worried about myself! What will happen to *me* if he is injured – or worse?'

Ali Baba and Esme looked at each other, shocked by this selfishness. Then Ali Baba set out for the forest on one of his donkeys. He soon came across two of Cassim's own donkeys wandering loose and alone.

'Where is your master?' Ali Baba asked them – though they, of course, could not answer. Ali Baba tied the donkeys together and continued.

A little further on, he came to the rock with the cave. 'Cassim?' he called, searching all around it. 'Cassim?'

But there was no answer there either.

Ali Baba studied the ground for tracks. He found mostly hoof prints that might have come from Cassim's donkeys. Then he saw a drop of something that might have been blood, but the colour was too dark to be sure; what had been ruby red the day before had darkened to garnet overnight.

At last Ali Baba said, 'Open

sesame.' The cave door opened and – 'Cassim!'

There was his brother, lying dead inside the entrance.

Although they were no longer close, Ali Baba had once loved his brother. It was this past love that made him cry now, especially as he wrapped Cassim's broken body in fine fabric and laid it across one of the donkey's backs. But it was his kind heart that made Ali Baba pause and look back at the treasure still crowding the cave.

Without a husband to work and support her, he thought, *Soraya will need her own money. I do not want her to be poor like I was …*

Quickly, Ali Baba loaded the second donkey with gold for Soraya. This time he did not have any chopped wood to cover the bags or Cassim's body with, so he

hid at the edge of the forest until nightfall. Then he rode the third donkey back to town.

He went straight to his sister-in-law's house, but it was the servant Morgiana who answered the door.

'I must see your mistress,' Ali Baba whispered.

'She has just gone to asleep,' Morgiana told him. 'I gave her some sleeping medicine. Perhaps I can help?'

Ali Baba hesitated. 'Do you promise to keep it a secret?'

Morgiana was a clever girl. Even before Ali Baba had mentioned

Cassim, she had noticed the bundle draped over one donkey. Although the body looked strange and misshapen, she could guess from a growing blood stain on the side nearest to her what it was. And she liked Ali Baba, who had always been kinder to her than his brother or Soraya.

'I promise,' she said.

'I bring with me your dead master's body. Will you help me to bury it?'

'We cannot bury him without a funeral,' Morgiana said. 'That will look suspicious. First we should start a rumour that he is ill–'

'But we cannot have a funeral,' Ali Baba insisted. 'If anyone sees the body, they will know that he did not die from natural causes.'

'Carry him into the house so that I can see what really happened.'

Ali Baba carried Cassim into the house, and Morgiana saw the true cause of his death.

'You are right,' she gasped, quietly horrified. 'No one must see the body like this.'

'Then we bury him?'

Morgiana thought for a moment. 'I have a better idea …'

Morgiana went out early the next morning. At the apothecary, she asked for medicine for her master.

'What is wrong with him?' asked the shopkeeper.

'At first it was just a cough,' said Morgiana. 'You remember the sleeping medicine you gave me for my mistress yesterday? That was to help her sleep through his coughing. But now it is worse.

apothecary
Someone who sells or prepares medicines, now called a pharmacist. Also the name of the place where medicines are sold or prepared, now called a pharmacy.

He cannot eat or sleep.'

The shopkeeper gave Morgiana some medicine and she took it away. But later that afternoon, she went back to the apothecary again.

'My master is worse!' she cried. 'He cannot seem to see or hear us. I need the strongest medicine you have – although I fear it will not save him.'

All that day, Ali Baba

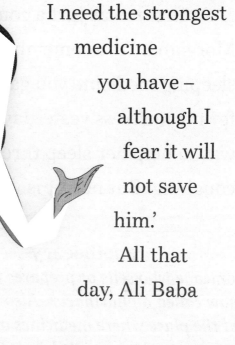

and his wife had been seen going in and out of Cassim's house with sad, serious faces. None of the neighbours were surprised when night fell and they suddenly heard a woman screaming.

'Cassim must be dead,' they said. 'Poor Soraya,' they said. 'She actually sounds upset!'

In fact until that moment, Soraya had been kept asleep. She was only now learning what had happened.

'What will I do?' Soraya wailed. 'What will I do without my husband? Who will look after me?

I am ruined!'

While Esme put an arm around her, it was on the tip of Ali Baba's tongue to mention the gold he had taken just for Soraya. But Morgiana shook her head. 'We need her grief to look real,' she had explained. 'She may not cry for a dead husband, but she will cry for lost money.'

And cry Soraya did. *Loudly.*

Chapter 3

By morning the whole town knew that Cassim was dead and were expecting his funeral to follow shortly. For the next part of her plan, Morgiana went to a cobbler called Baba Mustapha.

'Good morning,' she greeted him.

Baba Mustapha was old and grey. His eyesight had been fading for years, but he continued to mend

cobbler
A person who makes and fixes shoes.

shoes and sew leather by touch. Despite this, most of his customers now went to a younger cobbler.

'What do you want?' he asked Morgiana gruffly.

'I need you to mend something for me, if you are not too busy. It is a special project in need of special skill.'

The old man blushed slightly, pleased to have his abilities recognised for a change. 'What is this project?'

'If I tell you, I am afraid you will be put off by how difficult it is.'

Baba Mustapha scoffed. 'Nothing is too difficult for me! I have been mending things since long before you were born.'

'Forgive me. Perhaps that was not the right word. I simply worry that you will be too … *afraid*. Like the other cobbler.'

'The other cobbler? Hah! He is too young to know how it feels to stare death in the eye each day like I do! I am not afraid of death, so why should I be afraid of whatever you need me to mend?'

'Well, you see they are one and the same,' said Morgiana. 'Because I need you to sew a dead body back together.'

Baba Mustapha blinked in surprise.

'And I need you to do it blindfolded,' Morgiana added. She

knew that the cobbler's eyesight was bad, but she needed to make certain that he would not see anything.

For several moments, the cobbler did not reply. Then, 'In all my years, *that* is not something I have been asked to do before ...'

'And will you?' Morgiana added.

'Did you kill this person?'

'No. Nor did his family, who will pay handsomely for your help.'

'How handsomely?'

Morgiana named a sum of money that made Baba Mustapha's bleary eyes bulge. Still the old cobbler pretended to think about his answer.

'Very well,' he agreed at last.

After Baba Mustapha had fetched his sewing tools, Morgiana blindfolded him and led him to the house of the late Cassim. Her master's body had been so badly damaged by swords that it was in several pieces, as she proceeded to show the cobbler.

'You need to sew here,' said Morgiana. 'And here ... and–'

'Leave me alone, girl! I know what to do.'

Using his hands to feel his way, the cobbler got to work. Slowly but surely, stitch by stitch, he sewed the body back together. Afterwards

Baba Mustapha touched Cassim's face and tried to make out the features with his fingers.

'Who is he?'

Morgiana pulled the old man gently away. 'I cannot tell you.' She gave him a whole gold coin for his sewing. 'And I hope that you will not tell anyone else what happened here.' She gave him *another* coin for his secrecy.

When the cobbler was safely home again with his riches, Morgiana returned to wash the body and Ali Baba burned incense to perfume it. Finally, they wrapped the body in clean white sheets, just in time for the neighbours to arrive and help carry it to the burial ground. Prayers were said, and Cassim was laid to rest without anyone ever knowing the truth of how he died.

A few days after the funeral, Ali Baba and Esme moved into Cassim's house. This was expected

incense
A substance that makes a nice smell when burnt.

by everyone except Soraya.

'Why do you have to live with me?' she demanded angrily.

'Because you are my brother's widow,' answered Ali Baba. 'I have a responsibility to care for you now that he is gone.'

'I do not need you! I have the money from the cave.'

Once her tears had played their part, Ali Baba had told Soraya about the extra gold he took from the cave for her. Now he added, 'But how will you explain all your money to people with no one here

widow
A woman whose husband has died.

to run Cassim's business?'

Soraya laughed. 'Are you saying that *you* will run it instead? You are a woodcutter, not a merchant!'

'My son, Salil, is returning. He will run the business. He is clever enough.'

'Oh, so Salil will live here too? How wonderful!'

With this, Soraya stormed off to weigh her gold until she was calmer.

Elsewhere, in the forest, the forty thieves returned to their treasure. They were very unhappy to find that not only was the body of Cassim gone, so were two more bags of gold.

'That proves it,' said the leader: 'someone else knows about our hiding place.'

'What should we do?' his men wondered.

'Simple – we will find out who it is and kill him. I need a volunteer–'

Thirty-nine hands shot straight up into the air.

'– to go into town to see what you can learn. If you fail to find the thief, I will kill you in his place–'

Hands began lowering.

'– so only the best and bravest of us will do.'

At the end of this speech, there was only one hand still raised. It belonged to a man named Adeem who, despite being a thief himself, was particularly angry about being robbed.

Adeem disguised himself as a

traveller and went into the town where Ali Baba lived, which was the town closest to the forest in any direction. After days of searching and eavesdropping, he had not heard of anyone coming into sudden money, but he had worn through his right shoe.

Early one morning, before even the sun was truly awake, Adeem came across Baba Mustapha's stall. The old cobbler was already there with a stitching tool in his hand, working away.

'Honest sir,' Adeem greeted him, 'I have need of your services. But

I fear it is not yet light enough for you to see properly.'

'I do not need the light,' Baba Mustapha informed him, 'I have

my hands, and many *many* years of experience.'

Adeem handed over his shoe doubtfully. At first he watched Baba Mustapha squint as if he could not see a thing. Then he watched his wrinkled fingers move so quickly to mend the sole of his shoe that they were almost a blur.

'Not only do you not need the light, I suspect you could do this work blindfolded!' Adeem said.

Baba Mustapha cackled. 'This and more!' he agreed. 'Why just the other day I sewed a dead body back toge–'

Abruptly the old cobbler remembered his promise to Morgiana and stopped talking. Adeem leant closer with interest. He remembered Cassim's body and how it had been cut to pieces when he tried to escape.

'A *dead body*?' the thief echoed. 'Is that what just you said?'

'No, no.' Baba Mustapha shook his head fiercely. 'I said I could do my work *deaf to boot*.'

'I have no doubt that you could,' Adeem praised him. 'But I do not think that is what you said. Come

---

to boot
A casual way of saying 'also'.

now – do not be ashamed, for I am greatly impressed. You sewed a dead body together? Blindfolded? Amazing!'

Baba Mustapha said nothing, but his blush of pride gave him away.

'Tell me, where was this?' Adeem asked.

'I cannot.'

'I promise your secret is safe with me.'

'No, I mean I *cannot* tell you. I was blindfolded, remember? I did not see my way there or back.'

Adeem was thoughtful. 'I can see you are wise and clever.

I bet you remember some of the journey, do you not?'

'Why would I tell you?'

Adeem was in the process of taking money from his purse to pay for the shoe repair. As the sun came up it glinted off the gold coin he held up to the cobbler.

'Because I will pay you,' he said. When Baba Mustapha still hesitated, Adeem held up a second coin. 'Handsomely ...'

Another two gold coins was too much for Baba Mustapha to resist. He took the money and let himself be blindfolded again to recreate the conditions of his previous journey.

'First we went straight ...' he said. 'Then left, then left again – no, *right* – then straight for about a minute, then left down some steps, right – yes, I remember these cobbles ...'

Like this, the cobbler led the thief to Cassim's house, where Ali Baba now lived. But when Baba Mustapha took off the blindfold, he did not know either of those names, because this was not his neighbourhood.

'I do not know who lives here,' was all he could say when Adeem asked.

'Never mind,' said Adeem, 'my curiosity is satisfied. Please do not let me keep you any longer.'

As Baba Mustapha left for his stall, Adeem picked up a soft red stone from the ground and used it to chalk a cross onto the door of the house. Then he returned to the forest, and to a hero's welcome from his fellow thieves.

Chapter 4

A little after the cobbler and the thief parted ways, Morgiana went out of Ali Baba's house on an errand. As she closed the door, she noticed the mark Adeem had made upon it.

It is probably just children playing, she thought to herself. *But just in case ...*

She picked up the same soft red stone and used it to mark all of their neighbours' doors in the same manner. Then she went about her business.

In the forest, the thieves had listened to Adeem's story, congratulated him on his success and were now planning their next move. The leader said, 'We have no time to lose. This time we will all go into town, armed but disguised. We cannot go together for there are too many of us to go unnoticed. We will go in ones or twos and meet at the town square.

Adeem and I will go first.'

While the other thieves trickled more slowly into town, Adeem took the leader straight to the house with the marked door.

'You see?' he said proudly. 'I marked it so that we could find it again.'

'What about this one?' said the leader, pointing at the house next to it. 'It has the exact same mark. So does that one ... and that one ...' And as the leader continued to look around them, he realised something: 'They are *all* marked!'

'I-I do not understand,' said

Adeem, looking at the identical doors. 'I swear I only marked one!'
'You idiot!'

The leader was furious about this complication. Without knowing which house to target, he had no choice but to meet the rest of the thieves in the town square as planned and send them back to the forest. There, as promised, Adeem was beheaded for his failure, and the forty thieves became thirty-nine.

'Now,' said the leader, as Adeem's body was taken away. 'I need *another* volunteer.'

This time, not surprisingly, only one hand went into the air.

'You have a plan, Yusef?'

Yusef, whose hand it was, nodded. But being a thief, his plan was simply to steal Adeem's plan, which he did. He went into town dressed as a traveller as Adeem had done. He saw Baba Mustapha as Adeem had done. He paid Baba Mustapha to lead him to Ali Baba's house as Adeem had done. But there, instead of marking it with red chalk as Adeem had done, he marked it with …

Red *paint.*

When Morgiana saw the paint, she thought, *It is definitely* not *children making these marks, so …*

And she went to fetch some
water with which to wash the
paint away, ruining
the thieves' plans
yet again.

Back in the
forest, Yusef
met the
same fate as
Adeem and
the thirty-
nine thieves
became
thirty-eight.
'I need ...'
the leader

began, as Yusef's body was taken away. But he soon realised that his men were now more likely to cut off their hands than raise them to volunteer. 'Never mind,' he sighed. 'I will do it myself.'

The leader, who had stolen so many names he no longer remembered his real one, came to Ali Baba's house the same way that Adeem and Yusef had done. Baba Mustapha now had so much gold that he began to wonder whether he should retire.

The leader did not make any

retire
To stop working, usually later in life.

mark upon Ali Baba's door, either in chalk or paint or blood. He simply stared at it and the rest of the house until he had it memorised. Then he went away again, but not before Morgiana had seen him from the window.

There have been a lot of strange men about town recently, she thought. *I wonder what they are here for ...*

The leader told his men to buy nineteen mules, with thirty-eight large leather jars, one full of oil and the others empty. Each mule was to be loaded with two jars, one on each side of them for balance.

'Now what?' asked the thieves when they had done this.

'Get in,' said the leader.

'Get in what?'

---

mule
A cross between a donkey and horse. Mules are bigger than donkeys and stronger than horses.

The leader closed his eyes and counted to forty. *'Get. In. The. Jars.'*

Reluctantly – and for the larger thieves *painfully* – thirty-seven men squeezed themselves and their weapons into the jars. Afterwards the leader sealed the jars shut, leaving only a small air

hole for them to breathe. Then he changed into the clothes of a merchant. Disguised, he led his men into town, arriving after nightfall, and stopping outside Ali Baba's house. The leader knocked on the door, then kicked one of the jars which appeared to be groaning.

'Quiet!' He told the poor thief inside it, who had been sitting on his own arrows for hours.

'Sorry!' he whimpered. 'Is it time?'

'Nearly,' the leader promised.

Ali Baba answered the door and

the leader said, 'Good evening. I am sorry to disturb you so late at night. I have come a long way and I cannot find anywhere to stay at this hour. May I sleep here?'

Although Ali Baba had seen the leader of the thieves in the forest once, he did not recognise him in the clothes of a merchant. And although he had heard him speak before, too, he had not sounded like he did now. He sounded … *trustworthy*.

'Of course you can sleep here,' Ali Baba said kindly. 'I will just open the gate so that you can bring your mules into our courtyard.' As the animals were unloaded and taken to the stable, Ali Baba asked, 'What is it you have to sell? Oil?'

'The best,' said the leader of the thieves. And he opened the one jar containing oil to show him.

'Oh, perhaps my son, Salil, will want to buy some. He is the businessman of the family.

Morgiana?' he called. 'I know it is late, but could you bring us a little supper? Perhaps some soup? It is a little chilly tonight! Oh, and invite Salil to join us.'

As late as it was, the evening ran later. Ali Baba and Salil made the most of having company, and the three men talked until midnight.

By then the lamps had begun to flicker as the oil ran out.

'I think that means it is time to go to bed!' said Ali Baba.

At last! thought his guest, who let himself be led to an empty bedroom and pretended to go to sleep in it. In reality he would wait for his hosts to go to bed so that he could fetch his men and attack them.

'Goodnight, Morgiana,' said Salil, smiling warmly at her. 'I am sorry we kept you up so late. You must be tired.'

Indeed Morgiana *was* tired, but

one look from Salil was enough to make her forget it.

'Goodnight,' she said, smiling back.

As Morgiana tidied up in the kitchen, the lamp got dimmer and dimmer and finally went out. With no more oil in the house, or candles, Morgiana decided to help herself to some of the merchant's oil from the courtyard. In the dark, she tripped and fell against one of the jars.

'Sorry!' said a pained voice.

Morgiana froze. *That sounded like there is a man inside this jar ...*

'Is it time?' the voice came again.

There is a man inside this jar!

Out loud, but in a deeper voice than her normal one, she said, 'Erm, nearly.' Curiously she went through the other jars, tapping each with her foot, hearing and answering the same question thirty-six more times: 'Is it time?'

'Nearly.' 'Is it time?' 'Nearly.'

There are men in all *these jars,* she realised. *Could they be the ones I have seen about town recently?*

Quickly she used the oil to light her lamp and returned to the kitchen.

What should I do? she thought. *Ali Baba's room is right next to the guest room. If I try to tell him of this, the merchant will surely overhear and try to kill him. Perhaps he means to kill Salil too.*

Morgiana's eyes fell on the pot of soup cooling over the fire. It gave her an idea. True, it was a horrifying idea, but it was the only one she had that could deal with the men in the jars quickly and quietly.

Morgiana emptied the pot of soup and went back to fetch the jar of oil. She rolled it into the kitchen and set about boiling it in the cooking pot. This she had to do in batches because the cooking pot was smaller than the jar. She took each batch of boiling oil to the courtyard and emptied them down the airholes of each jar. The men inside them died instantly.

Then she went to her bedroom and watched from her window to see what the oil merchant did next, assuming he was not really a merchant at all.

Deciding that the rest of the house was asleep, the leader of the bandits went to his own window and began throwing stones at the jars in the courtyard below.

Each one struck its target with a low *ching* sound. This was the men's signal to climb out of their prisons. But they did not.

'Idiots!' the leader hissed. He was forced to creep out of his room and down to the courtyard in person. With a knife in each hand he kicked the jars. But no voices emerged.

'It is time!' he hissed.

But there was no answer.

Frowning, the leader removed the lid from one jar and saw that the man inside it was dead – as were the other thirty-six, he soon discovered. The plan had failed – *again*.

Morgiana watched as the leader (who no longer had anyone left to lead) stamped his feet and tore at his hair in frustration. Finally, he climbed the courtyard wall and fled.

Good riddance, Morgiana thought. Then she yawned, and finally went to bed.

Chapter 5

It was not until the next morning that Morgiana told Ali Baba and Salil what had happened. And it was not until she had shown them the inside of the jars that they believed her. Ali Baba was horrified. Salil was impressed.

'How clever you are!' he praised her.

'But what do we do now?' cried Ali Baba. 'There are thirty-seven dead men here, plus the oil merchant who got away, which makes thirty-eight. Two are missing but I can only assume that these are the same thieves whose gold I took from the cave and that the merchant is their leader. What if he returns to get revenge?'

'We will warn him not to,' said Salil.

'How?'

'The same way he warned you back at the cave: we will leave him a message ...'

Meanwhile, the former leader of

the forty dead thieves had locked himself in the cave of treasures. At least while he was there he could make sure no more of it was stolen. It was all his now because there was no one left to share it with.

What a bloodthirsty man that Ali Baba is, he thought. *To smile at me over supper while plotting mass murder! Or was it his son who did it?*

In the end he decided it did not matter: he would have to take revenge on Ali Baba's whole family. With his mind made up he left the cave and promptly tripped over the bodies of his men. Salil had returned them to the cave entrance. And while they had not been cut into pieces as Cassim had been, the message was the same: STAY AWAY.

For a long while it seemed like the thief had done as he was told. Time passed and the town was quiet. Even Morgiana's sharp eyes could not see anything to worry about. Under Salil's care, Cassim's business grew. And while Soraya was as mean as ever, the rest of the family were kind enough that their neighbours were happy for their success.

One day Salil met another merchant named Cogia Houssain and the two became friends.

Cogia was a thin, hunched man with a clean-shaven face who sold silks and carpets for a living – the finest silks and carpets Salil had ever seen in his life.

'I can see I have much to learn from you about quality!' said Salil.

'You are young,' Cogia replied. 'You have plenty of time to learn, and I would be glad to teach you.'

The older man was true to his word. He taught Salil everything he could. He always seemed to know where to find the best goods to buy and the richest people to sell them to. Salil was so grateful for his help that he introduced him to his father.

'You must be Ali Baba!' said Cogia warmly. 'Thank you for inviting me to your home.'

'I am the one who should be thanking you for all you have done for my son! This is my wife, Esme. And this is my sister-in-law, Soraya.'

'I was sorry to hear about your husband's death,' Cogia told Soraya. 'And you must be, Morgiana!' Cogia turned to the servant in the room. 'I have heard all about you.' He winked at Salil who blushed bright red. But Morgiana was frowning.

'Have we met?' she asked him.

'I am sure I would remember! Salil will tell you that I have an excellent eye for beauty – as does he.' Salil blushed again, and the family and their guest sat down.

Morgiana continued to stare at Cogia as she served. She noticed

as he drank that the bottom half of his face was paler than the top half. When he helped himself to nuts from the table, his fingers were scarred. And when he threw the stones from dried dates into the fire, they found their target every time.

In a flash, Morgiana remembered the so-called oil merchant who had once come to kill Ali Baba. She remembered his bearded face and the knives in his hands. She remembered him throwing stones at the jars where his men had been hidden.

It is the same man! she realised. *Cogia is the leader of the forty thieves!*

He might be thinner and hiding his height by hunching over, but Morgiana was sure of it. Looking again, she could even see the bulk of two knives under his tunic.

Unfortunately, once again, she could not say anything without putting the family in more danger. All she could do was wait until they were finished eating. Then she changed into a dress that Salil had given her, which was made with the brightest of Cogia's silks. Around her waist she put a girdle of beads and bells. On her head she put a long, floaty veil. Then she brought Salil his pipe.

'You want me to play?' Salil asked.

'Oh, yes!' Cogia clapped his hands. 'I love music!' But really he was thinking that the movement and noise might finally give him the chance he needed to kill his enemies. After which he would take back his gold, and steal the money Salil had worked for honestly.

'Well, Morgiana loves dancing,' said Salil. 'Will you dance for us, Morgiana?' Which was exactly what she had hoped he would say.

The moment Salil started playing, Morgiana started dancing. Ali Baba even banged the table like a drum. As Morgiana spun, her veil flew around her. As she jumped, the bells at her waist jingled. She was a dazzling sight. So dazzling that Cogia drew his knives under the table and then kept them there just to watch her.

Morgiana spun faster, jumped closer. The silk of her dress

shimmered, her body twisted, her hand flew out – *and seized one of Cogia's knives.* By the end of the dance, it was buried in his chest.

'What have you done?' cried

Salil, staring at his dead friend.

'I have saved you from the same thief as before! See his chin? It is pale as if he once had a beard.'

'Many men shave their beards off!'

'But how many silk merchants have such scars?'

'What scars?'

Morgiana revealed Cogia's hands, one of which still clutched the other knife. *'Those scars!'*

Salil was silent and sad. Ali Baba was loud and grateful.

'You are no servant, Morgiana, you are an angel! Thank you!

From now on you are free to do and go wherever you want. We are your friends not your masters. And if you would only marry my son, I would gladly call you family.'

Morgiana thought for a moment. 'I have a better idea ...'

Two years later, the merchant business that had once belonged to Cassim was one of the largest and most successful in Syria. Morgiana had helped to make it that way, a businesswoman in her own right. Her partner Salil loved meeting new people to do business with, but it was Morgiana who could always tell whether they were trustworthy or not. As for Soraya, she was so obsessed with money that she made an excellent accountant.

Ali Baba and Esme lived happily ever after, although Ali Baba always wondered what had become of the other two thieves, Adeem and Yusef.

And Baba Mustapha never retired.

accountant
A person whose job is to keep records of money for people and businesses.